Copy Cat

Written by Olivia George
Illustrated by Brett Hudson

My First READER

children's press®

A Division of Scholastic Inc.
New York Toronto London Auckland Sydney
Mexico City New Delhi Hong Kong
Danbury, Connecticut

Library of Congress Cataloging-in-Publication Data

George, Olivia.
  Copy Cat / written by Olivia George ; illustrated by Brett Hudson.
     p. cm. — (My first reader)
  Summary: A kitten longs to be like the big cats until it finds something they can all do together.
  ISBN 0-516-24679-8 (lib. bdg.)   0-516-25113-9 (pbk.)
  [1. Cats—Fiction. 2. Stories in rhyme.] I. Hudson, Brett, ill. II. Title. III. Series.
  PZ8.3+
  [E]—dc22
                              2004000239

Text © 2004 Nancy Hall, Inc.
Illustrations © 2004 Brett Hudson
All rights reserved.
Published in 2004 by Children's Press, an imprint of Scholastic Library Publishing.
Published simultaneously in Canada.
Printed in the United States of America.

CHILDREN'S PRESS and associated logos are trademarks and or
registered trademarks of Scholastic Library Publishing. SCHOLASTIC and
associated logos are trademarks and or registered trademarks of Scholastic Inc.

1 2 3 4 5 6 7 8 9 10 R 13 12 11 10 09 08 07 06 05 04

Note to Parents and Teachers

Once a reader can recognize and identify the 48 words used to tell this story, he or she will be able to successfully read the entire book. These 48 words are repeated throughout the story, so that young readers will be able to recognize the words easily and understand their meaning.

The 48 words used in this book are:

all	climb	get	lots	that
and	copy	go	me	the
are	day	grow	of	there
away	do	have	play	they
be	doing	hugs	purr	to
big	eat	I	room	want
call	everyone	is	say	what
can	for	it	small	you
cat	from	jump	so	
cats	fun	like	stretch	

Big cats have lots of fun all day.

They jump and purr.

They play and play.

I want to jump and play like that.

The big cats call me "Copy Cat."

The big cats climb. I want to go!

I want to eat so I can grow.

I want to stretch and purr all day.

They say, "Copy Cat, go away!"

What can small cats like me do?

Small cats can get hugs from you.

What are they doing? Can it be?

24

The big cats want to copy me!

Hugs from you are lots of fun.

There is room for everyone!

ABOUT THE AUTHOR

Olivia George was born and raised in Brooklyn, New York, and has spent her entire life surrounded by children's literature. She is, among other things, a childcare provider, a freelance editor and, of course, an author. Olivia has had many cats in her life, and one of her favorite activities is watching them play and interact with one another. She lives in Oakland, California, with her very own copy cat, Lola.

ABOUT THE ILLUSTRATOR

Brett Hudson graduated from Southampton University in 1997. Since then, he has illustrated many books for all age groups in addition to producing greeting cards and working on a medical magazine. In his spare time, Brett enjoys playing soccer and going to the movies. He and his partner, Lindsey, live near the sea in sunny Brighton, England.